For the Truth Seekers

Sahar Hadid

THE WAKING CRESCENT

AUSTIN MACAULEY PUBLISHERS™
LONDON • CAMBRIDGE • NEW YORK • SHARJAH

Copyright © Sahar Hadid 2023

The right of Sahar Hadid to be identified as author of this work has been asserted by the author in accordance with Federal Law No. (7) of UAE, Year 2002, Concerning Copyrights and Neighboring Rights.

All rights reserved. No part of this publication may be reproduced, stored in a retrieval system, or transmitted in any form or by any means, electronic, mechanical, photocopying, recording, or otherwise, without the prior permission of the publishers.

Any person who commits any unauthorized act in relation to this publication may be liable to legal prosecution and civil claims for damages.

This is a work of fiction. Names, characters, businesses, places, events, locales, and incidents are either the products of the author's imagination or used in a fictitious manner. Any resemblance to actual persons, living or dead, or actual events is purely coincidental.

The age group that matches the content of the books has been classified according to the age classification system issued by the Ministry of Culture and Youth.

ISBN 9789948802273 (Paperback)
ISBN 9789948802280 (E-Book)

Application Number: MC-10-01-4792762
Age Classification: 13+

First Published 2023
AUSTIN MACAULEY PUBLISHERS FZE
Sharjah Publishing City
P.O Box [519201]
Sharjah, UAE
www.austinmacauley.ae
+971 655 95 202

Acknowledgements

Thank you to Arlene Clark, my high school English teacher of four years, who sparked my interest in teaching and writing. Who knew a decade later you would be the first person to read and edit my first book! I am forever grateful for your guidance and gracious teaching methods and for your overall role in my life. I owe a chunk of my writing skills to what I developed in your class.

Thank you to my younger sister, Yassmina Hadid, who not only encouraged me throughout my writing journey, but also gave me valuable bird-eye view feedback. You helped me see my book from a different perspective, which allowed me to cater to a wider audience.

Thanks, Pops, for your unconditional support and patience. You accepted and embraced the chaos that came at a time when I felt lost while trying to find my passion. You wholeheartedly supported me when I finally discovered and followed my passion for writing.

Auntie Susu I'm forever grateful to you and proud to be named after you. You have always supported me and pushed me to do the things I believed in. You gave me a loving and nurturing space to grow from which taught me how to draw my own conclusions and to find my own solutions to problems I faced. You guided me to listen to the voice within myself, which I learned to express through writing.

Boudikins thanks to your graphic skills, my book cover was created! I couldn't envision it until you created a sample which captured the essence of my book in a simple way. It has also set the tone for all my future books. I'm forever grateful for your contribution to my book and life in general!

I'm grateful to Austin Macauley Publishers for believing in my first book. With your help and appreciation, my google docs manuscript manifested into a book! Thank you to all the different departments that were involved.

I must mention Paulo Coelho and JK Rowling as their books on alchemy have helped me not only with this book, but on my own journey. I'm grateful to have come across their work during specific moments in my life where they were able to indirectly guide me and enlighten me through their words.

Text from the Emerald Tablet also known as the Smaragdine Tablet or Tabula Smaragdina has been quoted in the book.

Part 1

Chapter 1

Kaya was curled up on the sand dune by the sycamore tree where she would often lie watching the sun set behind her town with her husband.

She hugged her knees tightly while looking out at her drowning village. The fear in her light-brown eyes reflected in her horse's.

Where do we go now?

She'd been rocking since the river engulfed her village. The yearly flooding had been a blessing, creating the rich, dark soil that gave the land the name *Kemet,* meaning The Black Land; only this time, the flooding had been unforgiving. The calamity had left only Kaya and her horse Orion alive.

Although Kaya didn't know what lay outside the collapsed Syenite granites, she did know that she needed to make a move before the sun set.

Vast and empty, the desert seemed endless as they trailed along the grained path. Trudging ahead, she kept with her only memories from her past.

"Wake up Kaya. It's a beautiful day. You have another life to sleep."

She remembered how she would wake up to Arius staring lovingly at her with his green hooded eyes. He would rise at dawn while she slept till the early afternoon.

Is it fair that I wake here while he lies sleeping? The wakeful one asleep, she thought, staring at the bleak path ahead.

Orion trod sluggishly on.

*

Up ahead, the sound of the streaming water rippled them both back to awareness. Orion approached the tireless bed of water and took long gulps. Kaya climbed down, grabbed two blankets from the saddlebags and placed them on the grass near a willow tree.

The night before, she had packed the saddlebags for Arius' yearly journey to Alexandria. Kaya had walked with him outside the city walls as she usually did before his departure.

Why did he go back to the house? What did he forget? If he hadn't gone back, he would've been with me.

The thought of that sent streams of her own down her face. Her heart was heavy with grief, sadness and loneliness.

She hadn't noticed the time passing. The sun had almost set over the river.

She walked towards the river, cupped water between her hands washing it over her tired face. She took a few sips, not having had anything to eat or drink since the catastrophe at dawn.

She grabbed a lotus essential oil from another saddlebag, unclipped her himation, a robe attached at the top of one shoulder, slipped off her chiton, a long white tunic, then dipped into the river. She rubbed the oil between her palms creating a foamy lather then scrubbed it lightly and gently over her skin as if she were a delicate child. She rolled her head back loosening her long brown hair into the water and tenderly massaged her scalp. The memory of Arius massaging her scalp with his strong yet gentle hands sent her out of the water feeling light-headed.

She patted the water drops dry with a light cloth then put on a white linen himation which had belonged to Arius, catching a whiff of his scent.

She set their communion blanket on top of the thicker one in an attempt to create a place of comfort. The communion blanket had a print of the lotus flower Arius had given her. In their village, the men gave their bride-to-be a flower as a symbol of their commitment. If the women accepted it, that bonded the man and woman as one. They were in communion. Kaya had sewn that quilt the day of their wedding. The flower that wed them, bed them. She sat on it uncomfortably realizing that she would never share it with him again.

She forced a grape into her mouth despite feeling nauseous at the mere thought of eating. Giving up, she closed her eyes and cocooned herself in the blanket feeling scared yet too drained to give in to the panic.

Orion suddenly neighed.

Kaya's eyes shot open releasing the suppressed panic. The starry moonless night comforted her as her gaze fixated on the darkness that blanketed piercing little lights. One in particular was shining extra bright.

Arius would say, "All life comes from Source and returns to Source." They believed that they came from the brightest star in the night sky, Sirius, an oceanic land filled with blue water and glowing spirit-like figures. Lightspirits. And that was where their souls would return.

Kaya wondered whether that was where he had returned to as she shivered under her blanket, wrapping her arms around herself as if it were Arius' veiny arms around her, ensuring the warmth of her blanket wasn't the only thing hugging her.

Sirius twinkled, igniting a smile on her face while lightening the load on her eyes and heart. She imagined Lightspirits dancing in the dry, cold night. Dancing in commemoration.

*

Kaya's eyes swung wide open. She could see the starry night above her, but couldn't turn her face left or right. She tried lifting her body up, but couldn't move at all. From the corner of her eye, she saw the silhouette of her husband. A wave of water came towards them engulfing him. He was drowning as she lay next to him untouched. She couldn't yell. She couldn't run. She couldn't move. She couldn't help him. The more she panicked, the more her body froze. She realized she was sleeping yet awake. She closed her eyes tightly and opened them again hoping to wake up only to find herself still stuck in her nightmare. She tried to open and close her eyes again, but to no avail. For the third time, she closed her eyes, inhaled deeply and counted backwards from five. She opened her eyes to the dark wilderness around her gasping for air. Unable to keep her eyes open, Kaya fell asleep again, her thoughts still wide awake and racing with worry, her breath the only constant.

In and out.

In and out.

Chapter 2

Kaya woke up to a high-pitched wailing amidst the suffocation of the sun. Orion, now also awake, let out a disgruntled moan. Looking around and above, Kaya tried to spot the creature.

An eagle was gliding towards the north. Kaya took note of the welcoming path to the left of the upstream river and decided to move in that same direction, for in their culture, an eagle signified protection and rebirth.

At least it knows where it's going.

The orange light had dispelled the once dark night. She packed up her things, refilled her waterskin, hopped on Orion, and headed out on a directed yet directionless journey, choosing to believe she was being guided.

Arius always talked about his ventures outside of the village. He was in search of The Truth. "An experienced, untaught Truth. A feeling, a knowing of something greater, bigger yet unknown." She recollected the way he ran his fingers through her hair as he spoke passionately.

He was right about the greater and bigger.

*

The river was no longer visible as they ventured into the red-colored sand.

Orion let out a signaling neigh, rising up slightly on his hind legs as if pointing towards something with his front ones.

It was a someone.

An older man with a neat white beard and curly short grey hair sat cross-legged on a reed mat wearing a white linen knee-length chiton. Behind him was a mud brick house.

Orion approached the old man as if he knew him. The old man was biting into an apple before he looked up and smiled.

"Kaya, you're here."

Kaya wasn't sure if she had heard him correctly given her state of fatigue and numbness. The old man picked up a stick, plummeting half his weight to one side and the rest onto his hand, pushing off the ground to stand on his feet. He walked towards Orion, fed him the rest of his apple, then stroked his muzzle. Kaya noticed the wrinkles at the edges of his deep, sympathetic blue eyes.

"Orion loves his apples," he said.

She didn't make much of it. Perhaps her husband had met him before.

"Have you met Arius?"

"Come with me," he replied and turned to walk towards the adobe house.

She jumped off Orion who had at first sight happily succumbed to following the old man.

Thinking they were walking to the mud-brick house, Kaya was perplexed when they walked past it leaving behind the red sand. They entered a grass area where there was a pond surrounded by bushes and flowers which were in turn fortified by trees.

The old man took Orion from Kaya and left him near a shaded tree with a barrel of water where he could graze. He then grabbed a torch and led Kaya into a cave down a stone staircase.

They entered a narrow hall where there were torches hung on sconces along the walls providing light. As they walked deeper into the cave, the space grew wider with a few klines, wooden reclining couches with a headboard, aligned by the wall. There were cushions and linen neatly placed on them. There were also fresh barrels of fruits, vegetables and wheat.

"Help yourself, please. You must be hungry from traveling."

Kaya scooped up some cherries and popped them into her mouth.

The old man politely signaled her to sit down on a kline near the barrels. It felt cool there.

From a distance, she could hear what sounded like a waterfall yet was unable to see where the sound was coming from.

"Arius told me you would be coming soon."

"How do you know Arius?" she asked, suddenly curious about their connection.

She was happy to meet someone that knew her husband but felt slightly irritated, wondering why Arius had never mentioned this man to her.

"You must have a lot of questions, but I've been holding on to this for you."

He walked towards the grayish cave walls, bent down using his stick and then pulled out a loose brick at the bottom of the wall. He grabbed the hidden letter that was tucked away, and handed it to Kaya before putting what felt like a consoling hand on her shoulder. Then he silently made his way back up the stairs.

When he was out of sight, Kaya looked down at the letter, picking at the seal.

She finally decided to open it feeling something heavy inside. She reached for the object. It was a necklace similar to her husband's made of linen thread with a copper symbol attached to it of the Flower of Life, a figure that had overlapping circles arranged in a flower pattern. Arius would talk about this symbol endlessly and how it signified one's journey from the Outer to the Inner.

She placed the necklace around her neck and proceeded to open the folded letter.

My Beloved Kaya,

I know you may feel lost, defeated and confused at this very moment.
But this is the beginning of your Inner Journey.
A journey that is taken within, will reflect the one ventured without.
It's yours and yours alone.
Trust what unfolds in front of you and follow your guides.
We are always around you and within you.
You will learn how to anchor yourself in times of distress.

Until we meet again,
Arius

She pulled her hair away from the tears on her cheeks with her letter in hand.

How'd he know that I would be alone? Why couldn't he have prepared me for all that was coming instead of writing a damn letter? I don't feel supported, guided or loved! I just want to be back home with my husband.

Kaya stared blankly at the cave wall as she played with the symbol around her neck. Her mind fell silent as she heard water gushing. Still wondering where the water was coming from, she placed the letter back into the envelope and left it on the kline.

She walked towards the sound and saw a wooden bridge leading to a rocky pedestal basin that was rooted within the ground.

She walked onto the bridge and peered down at the darkness that lurked below. Noticing where the sound of distant water was coming from, she quickly fixed her gaze on the pedestal in front of her, not daring to look down again.

Once she reached the end of the bridge, she walked towards the pedestal. The basin was almost filled with water.

Kaya stared down at her reflection and fixated on the ripples of water making out her features. She looked deep into her exhausted and puffy eyes, then at her small nose incapable of taking in another sniffle and finally at her hollow cheeks that had been plump just a few nights ago.

She wasn't blinking.

The more she fixated on her reflection, the more it blurred. The blurriness of her silhouette turned into a white figure. She continued staring at the figure which seemed to be glowing. When she blinked, the Lightfigure disappeared.

She stood there silently not wanting to question her sense of peace.

Feeling drawn to the water, Kaya brought her palms together collecting water and took a sip. A cleansing wave rushed through her.

She felt safe – tranquil.

Footsteps approached from behind her. When she turned around, she saw the old man. "What is this?" she asked, looking at the pedestal.

"The Elixir of Life. It purifies and fertilizes, planting seeds for creation. Come now. You'll need to rest before you continue on your journey tomorrow."

Although Kaya had more questions, she did feel tired from the unexpected events of the day and hadn't realized how many hours had passed while she was down there.

As she approached the kline, she spotted her arranged saddlebags.

"Thank you."

She softly smiled at him and he smiled back then exited the cave.

She removed her communion blanket from a saddlebag and retrieved a small leather pouch from the bottom. Her husband had used it to hold his gold while traveling. She placed the letter in the pouch and tucked it back into the bottom of the saddlebag near the lotus oil. She grabbed her communion blanket and tucked herself in.

Not seeing a hint of light from the entrance of the cave, she realized that it was dark outside. As soon as she heard Orion's neigh, her thoughts turned into nonsense, and she fell asleep.

Chapter 3

As the first streak of light struck the entrance of the cave, Kaya awoke. She had synced her sleep and wake cycle with the setting and rising of the sun.

When she stepped outside, she was welcomed by Orion who was drinking water. Near him were bundles of goods which she figured the considerate old man had packed for them.

She buckled the rest of their saddlebags onto Orion and they went on their way.

Continuing on her directionless yet directed journey, Kaya felt more confident than the morning before. Meeting the old man and receiving her husband's letter, gave her a sense of comfort. She realized that she wasn't alone.

*

The caramel-colored rays glistened on the path in front of them, blending with Orion's light-cream coat as they approached Hierakonpolis. The City of the Falcon. It was associated with Horus whose right eye represented the sun and left eye represented the moon.

"The coming together of the light and dark," Arius had told her.

There was a young woman standing near the river facing the mountains wearing a himation similar to Kaya's.

Her eyes were shut.

She bent one arm towards her chest drawing circles away from her, while her other hand overlapped circling in towards her. As she moved faster and faster, the heavy air seemed to collect particles, leaves and sand. She was in a serene trance-like state. As the rhythm of her hands slowed down, the once heavy air seemed to grow lighter.

As if having felt a presence, the young woman opened her eyes and turned to face Kaya. They regarded each other for a few moments.

She had amber almond-shaped eyes. Her gaze was tender and glistening. Her ginger hair was long and wavy, and her skin fair. Her full cheeks accentuated her heart-shaped lips.

"Have you just come from the cave?"

Distracted by the woman's performance, Kaya stared blankly at her not knowing what to make of the question.

The young woman pointed at Orion's hoof prints.

"The red sand there stains the hooves. It's the only sand like that out here."

Was the cave well-known?

"You've been to the cave as well?" Kaya asked.

"Every year on a Reconciliation Journey."

Kaya scrunched her brows in confusion so the young woman continued.

"My husband and I set off on separate journeys each year to reconnect with ourselves."

Did she know about the Elixir of Life?

"Where are you off to?" the woman continued, interrupting Kaya's train of thought.

"I'm not sure."

The young woman seemed to realize her question had saddened Kaya.

"Keep on that way," the young woman said, pointing away from the river. "You'll find a forest of Ished trees with a cabin. I'm Aura by the way."

"Kaya."

"I need to get going, but hopefully we'll meet again soon," Aura said with a genuine smile.

Kaya found herself trusting her guidance. Although she didn't know Aura, she felt a sense of comfort and familiarity, and not just because they had both experienced the cave.

Part 2

Chapter 4

As they blindly fought through bushes and tree branches, Kaya looked up at the crescent moon for guidance helping her eyes adjust to her surroundings.

A detritus-strewn pathway brought them to a rustic cabin that was encased within the roots of a tree. The tree's roots ran along the sides of the cabin with a stone well situated in front.

Kaya jumped off Orion, led him to the grass area and set out some extra apples for him. She used the bucket from the well to fill water for Orion who was already munching away at the apples.

She grabbed the saddlebag that had become her essential and made her way to the arched dark-blue door that had a lit torch placed in a sconce next to it.

She lifted the torch and knocked. No one answered.

Kaya knocked again and then slowly opened the door revealing a single room with a large cushion at the center and candles all around. There was a large rectangular bronze mirror against the wall facing the door. Ivy vines entangled the walls, ceiling, floor and the mirror. There was a sconce parallel to the outer one where Kaya placed the torch and near it a window.

She lay down on the cushion with her communion blanket and closed her eyes.

*

Kaya opened her misting eyes, disturbed by the sun's reflection in the mirror. She could see herself curled up in a fetal position. She noticed some writing on the mirror. Rubbing her eyes, she squinted trying to make out the words.

She walked towards the mirror and found a large tree engraved on it. The tree had names written on the branches and on the trunk was a poem:

Tree of Life

like the intricate branches of the tree,
we are all connected

She skimmed over the names on the branches and figured it was some sort of family tree. Some branches had single names; others were grouped together. A few names appeared much more distinctly than others.

Hecate

Gennadios, Maia
Kaya

Kepheus, Aura
Zotikos

Could Aura have a family? She was the one who sent me here.

She ran her fingers over the names then moved over to seven names grouped together, of which she noticed three in particular:

...Solon, Zosimos, Kaya

She looked back up at the first *Kaya,* placed within a family, and then back down at the second *Kaya,* placed amongst the group. She had never heard of any of the other names before.

Her gaze then shifted to a name right underneath the second Kaya, faded yet visible, which sent shivers down her spine and goosebumps across her arms and legs.

Arius

Her heart started racing. Her palms began to sweat. Her head pulsated with the beat of her heart. Her chest grew tight and her throat dry.

Kaya stepped away from the mirror and tripped backwards, falling onto the cushion bracing herself with her arms.

Feeling like the room's walls were closing in on her, she took deep breaths and closed her eyes. Her fingers raised towards her temples lightly massaging them. She felt the thoughts receding with each stroke. She continued inhaling and exhaling until her mind was empty of racing thoughts.

You are safe. You are guided. You are loved.

The mantras of an inner divine voice filled her now quieted mind. She wrapped her arms around her womb area and began to weep. And weep. And weep.

Until she was empty of tears.

She then rubbed her chest feeling peace and warmth radiating out of her heart through to the rest of her body.

She had released and self-soothed.

She stood up, walked towards the door and opened it allowing a rush of cool, fresh air to enter. The clouds were perfectly drawn onto the light-blue sky.

She saw Orion lying on the lush green grass as the aroma of yellow, white and red jasmine flowers nestled near the sides of the door filled the air.

Kaya grabbed her belongings and closed the door, which appeared light-blue in the morning sun, behind her.

She jumped on Orion feeling light and unburdened after releasing the weight off her chest. Although she had accumulated question upon question each day since the flood, she was slowly learning to accept the uncertainty that had previously only plagued her with anxiety.

From up above, there was that familiar screeching dragon noise. It was the eagle flying right above them. One of its brown feathers drifted down and landed on Orion's rump.

Like birds, humans shed as they grow, for casting off the old frees their once captured wings

Chapter 5

They approached Thebes and entered the bustle of the city which had a major road down the center with smaller, narrower streets connecting to it. The houses and buildings were made of mud-brick much like what Kaya was used to. The Temple of Karnak and the Temple of Luxor were connected by the Avenue of Sphinxes.

She felt overwhelmed and decided to walk beside Orion who was also uncomfortable. People swept by them hurriedly, shoving through unapologetically. One young woman however did turn around and apologize.

It was Aura.

"Kaya!" Aura yelped excitedly while hugging Kaya tightly. "I was hoping you'd make it here! Come with me!"

She grabbed Kaya's hand leading her hastily up narrower alleys that seemed to get less and less busy until they reached a picturesque home at the top of a hill. There were welcoming plants and flowers at the front of the house. At the back was a huge field with a fence down the middle, creating one space for the crops and another space for the horses and cattle.

A boy with curly ginger hair, the spitting image of Aura, came running towards the two wearing a cloth wrapped and fastened around his middle. A man plowing the field turned around at the sight of the boy running.

The boy wrapped himself around Aura and rested his head on her shoulder giving Kaya a glimpse of his amber eyes.

"Will you not introduce yourself to our guest, Zoti?"

He jumped out of her arms and approached Kaya with a charm-filled smile.

"I'm Zotikos. It's a pleasure to meet you," he said through rosy cheeks while putting out his hand for a gentleman-like handshake that made both Kaya and Aura giggle.

The man approached from behind Zotikos resting his hand on the boy's shoulder.

"He gets that from his dad," he said with a wink leaning forward to plant a kiss on Aura's cheek which showed his sharp jawline. His hazel eyes and blond hair glistened in the sun as he brushed his hair away from his golden skin. He was wearing only white linen pants showing off his fit build.

"I'm Kepheus."

Kaya froze, recollecting the names she had read on the mirror. She stared blankly at the man and boy in front of her, finding it strange that she had already known their names while just having met them.

"Can I introduce him to the other horses please?" Zotikos jumped up and down eagerly, snapping Kaya out of her thoughts.

"Sure," she replied with a reassuring smile.

Zoti skipped along with Orion, leading the way to the field.

"Come let me show you the house," Aura said, opening her hand out towards it.

The house had three spacious floors. The downstairs had a kitchen overlooking the field with a pass-through window where there were stools aligned along the outside. Upstairs there were three bedrooms.

"This one's yours! We'll be waiting for you on the roof for dinner!" Aura pointed to the staircase at the end of the hall.

Kaya nodded shyly with pursed lips, feeling as though she didn't have any say in the matter and yet satisfied with their manner.

Her room had a window facing the back of the house where she could see the field. Orion was running alongside two other horses.

She unpacked a few saddlebags and although she wouldn't be staying for long, it felt good to have a place to settle in for a few days. Living out of saddlebags had become tiresome.

*

Kaya heard some laughter from the third floor. She climbed up the stairs and onto the roof. The sun had almost completely set leaving hues of blue, purple and pink.

Torches lit each corner of the roof. There was a large cooking pot on a fire in the middle. Klines were placed along the walls and reed mats were spread around the floor. Kaya got a whiff of the stew brewing, a whiff she hadn't smelt since the night before Arius' departure. Zoti was sitting near Kepheus on a reed mat reading while Aura stirred the pot.

"Right on time!" Aura said as soon as she saw Kaya.

"I would ask if you needed help, but it seems I'm too late." Kaya smiled with her lips shut tightly sensing heat in her cheeks, feeling shy.

"All you need is your bowl!"

"Please help yourself with a drink as well!" Kepheus said, pointing at the selection of beer, red wine, fruit juices and water placed on a small wooden bench.

Kaya poured some wine and grabbed a bowl. Aura served some carrots, lentils and beef, pouring lemony-infused broth on top.

Kaya marveled at the all-encompassing city view, the miniature lit up rooftops. Families gathered together to share more than just heartful meals. She was grateful for the wonderfully loving people who had welcomed her into their home, making her feel like she was a part of their family, even if it was just momentary.

*

It was already past midnight. Zoti had fallen asleep on Kaya's lap to the sound of Aura's graceful voice harmonizing with Kepheus' lute. They had almost finished the jar of wine. Aura offered Kaya what would be her last kylix of wine before heading to bed.

Kaya felt the urge to ask them some questions, hoping they would be able to give her some answers.

"I came across that cabin you told me about," she said while brushing Zoti's hair gently with her hand. Reluctant to go to bed, her touch had placed him in the comfort of her lap.

Kepheus and Aura looked at Kaya as they cuddled together.

"Are those our names on the mirror?"

Aura nodded and said, "Yes. If you were able to enter the cabin, then your name must be there."

Kaya remembered seeing her name twice and was almost certain hers was the one near her late husband's.

"Why are they there? How are we all connected?"

"All the names written on the mirror have a common desire or purpose – connecting to their infinite source of love, light and peace, what some call The Truth, in order to spread it," Kepheus answered.

Kaya thought about his statement remembering her husband's quest for The Truth while also recalling her life-long prayer:

Finding love within, to spread without

"When you have faith, you trust, and when you trust, you allow the Source within you to become a Creator," Kepheus continued.

A Creator? Kaya thought to herself, feeling the wine going to her head and her eyes beginning to shut.

Aura smiled and said, "We have more time to talk. For now, let's go to sleep."

Kepheus picked up Zoti who was still asleep and wrapped him around his body. Kaya set down the bronze kylix and stumbled her way down to bed.

Chapter 6

Kaya woke a few hours after sunrise. She hadn't slept past sunrise since she was back home with her husband. She stretched her arms out over her head feeling rejuvenated. She saw the family sitting in the field outside her window. She tidied up then made her way out to the field.

On a blanket spread out over the grass, Zoti was reading aloud to Aura and Kepheus. The horses were loose around the green field. The pass-through window had a counter stacked with bread, jam, milk and tea.

"Oh, you're up!" Aura said seeing her. "We were starting to wonder whether we'd lost you to that bed!"

"Yeah I got a bit too comfortable in its captivity," Kaya laughed, feeling warm inside.

She helped herself to some breakfast then soaked in the fresh air while looking around at their land. The soil in the field was ready for seeding.

She spotted a wooden ladder leading up a tree.

"We built that before Zoti was born," Kepheus said, following her gaze. "Aura and I sit up there to watch the sunsets and sunrises. It has quite the view. We even catch Aurora's celestial lights. Do make sure to give it a look while you're here."

Kaya remembered the first day she had met Arius. They watched the rare neon greenish-yellow lightshow from what would become their hill. Arius told her that the magical lights would happen on the day they reunited in each lifetime. That it was him racing across the sky to reach her. That was the first and only time Kaya had seen the lights.

"Get ready Kaya, we're heading to the market!" Aura said with a beaming smile that matched her eyes as she stood up and pranced over to the side of the house.

Kepheus laughed at the evident hesitation in Kaya's face. "Brace yourself."

Kaya chuckled as Aura began making her way with a wagon dragging behind her.

*

As Kaya had dreaded, there were flocks of people bumping into each other in the outdoor marketplace. There were farmer stalls with vegetables, fruits, wheat, barley, geese, ducks, goats and cattle. Other stalls displayed crafts, such as jewelry, pottery, and furniture. One stand sold candles, tapestries, books and clothes. Kaya wandered over there looking through the different books.

There was a brown leather book titled The Tree of Souls which had been her favorite growing up. She had imagined Lightspirits within a glowing tree making their way through the trunk and out from the branches. She had read how those souls came to Earth in human form, spreading light and love, before returning home to their stars. She flipped to a poem in the book which read:

Dear Inner Child,

You came out exhilarant and ripe
Then grew to be disturbed with life
You appear sometimes in fight or flight
Projecting things when you don't feel right

Time and again your reactions show,
That this old way has no hold

Oh Child, Oh Child
But you've been bright,
Illuminating my way through the night

Although she had read the book countless times, the poem seemed unfamiliar to her.

She decided to get the book for the family as a gift. She also bought them a set of hugging candles in the shape of a man and a woman cradled together as one and a tapestry with a beige and white patterned Flower of Life. She bought herself a chiton, himation and undergarments.

As she left the market, she saw Aura in front of a stall trying to make space on the wagon by shoving all the goods she had bought together. She had bought a duck, fish, vegetables, fruits, beer, wine, linen, pillows and reed mats. It seemed like she was preparing for a feast.

*

When they arrived back at the house, Aura and Kepheus went for a nap, so Kaya decided to climb up the ladder that led to a spacious wooden box attached to the tree.

She climbed into the box, which had a reed mat and cushions, and dangled her feet from the opening at the front as she watched the orange sun setting behind the green hills. Birds were flying together, circling in a cone-shaped pattern.

Kaya wondered whether Arius was watching her. Sometimes she felt like an abandoned child – anxious, scared, always wanting to return home to him. But courage and growth came from no longer having that home to run to.

Like a newborn, born needy,
searching for a caretaker, a lover, outside
Until the seeker finds the lover within

The poem from The Tree of Souls had resonated with her.

She sat quietly inspecting the lands behind the land. Blanketed with familiarity in one moment, exposed to the unknown in the next. The thought of that used to frighten her, but she was now sitting here marveling at what would come next. She had recently caught herself contemplating excitedly the path ahead of her, proud that she had these moments where she was accepting moving forward without Arius.

Loud clacking, clunking and banging sounds came from the kitchen. Kaya presumed that they were beginning to cook and climbed down in a hurry to join them.

Aura was cutting some vegetables, while Kepheus prepped the duck. Kaya offered to make her famous pumpkin stew. Zoti set out the new mats on the roof floor and placed silver plates and cups.

*

"He was too shy to talk to me so he would leave a daisy on my window every night. But one day, my mother caught him trying to leave the flower and Kepheus, all flustered, hesitated and decided to give her the flower instead. My mom was confused thinking he was asking her to elope with him. She hadn't seen me hiding behind the door!" Aura was trying to enunciate her words as clearly as possible around her laughs.

"My mom was pleasantly shocked, flattered even. My dad on the other hand came out from behind her insulted and enraged. He could've killed him."

They all burst out laughing at the thought of Aura's father witnessing a handsome adolescent boy trying to lure his middle-aged wife away.

"Thankfully Aura came out of hiding finally accepting my flower and, needless to say, saved me from her father who was ready to lunge at me," Kepheus joined in.

As they shared their stories, Kaya's laughter turned into reminiscing. They noticed her now glum expression and grew silent.

"Have either of you met my husband?" Kaya asked hopeful, yet she also realized there was a possibility she would feel hurt if they had.

Kepheus was first to speak, "This time last year, I was on my Reconciliation Journey to the Elixir of Life when I bumped into a young man. He was leaving just as I was getting there. It seemed like it was his first time. He had the same confused yet tranquil expression that people have when they first leave. He told me his name was Arius and that he had a wife back in Syene."

Why does Kepheus, a stranger to my husband, know about me, while I, his wife, know nothing about who he had encountered or about his experience with the Elixir of Life? What else don't I know about? It's like he led a whole other life without me.

Kaya's thoughts triggered a tear down her face which she was quick to wipe away. In a failed attempt to shrug it off she asked Aura, "What were you doing by the river the first time I met you?"

Aura smiled knowing very well what Kaya was referring to. "Well, each of us has a sort of divine incarnation. When you sit with yourself and go within, you can tap into your inner gifts. These can be used to heal and align the body, mind and soul."

Kaya remembered when she had first heard the divine inner voice back at the cabin after seeing the names on the mirror.

"So that was my name among the group. Who are they?" Kaya asked, confused.

"That we don't know."

There was a moment of silence that filled the room with unanswered thoughts before Aura continued, "But Kaya, I do know this. Everything happens in divine timing. The Inner Journey is a hard path, but one that will liberate you. Trust it. It's yours and yours alone."

Kaya didn't know whether to feel blessed amidst her feelings of frustration and confusion. She felt overwhelmed, and once again, in the dark about her husband.

She went to bed twisting and turning with her racing thoughts. The words from her husband's letter riddled back to her, "It's yours and yours alone."

Part 3

Chapter 7

The next morning while everyone was still asleep, Kaya packed her things. She placed the gifts in the kitchen near the breakfast she had prepared for the family. She had learned how to make Teganitai, a sort of flat-cake, made out of wheat flour, honey, water and olive oil, from her Greek mother who had moved to Syene shortly after falling in love with her father, a pure Aswanian. Aswan had been the name of the city Syene prior to the Greeks taking over.

After the previous night, Kaya felt an urge to be on her way. Whenever she thought she was getting answers she ended up with more questions. She knew that she needed to be alone to figure out some answers for herself. She felt far away from herself, or maybe she was just getting to re-know herself. The only life that she had ever known had collapsed before her eyes and here she was trying to make sense of it while also trying to build a new life.

She set off on Orion and heard the now familiar shriek. There, up above, was her feathered traveling companion. She smiled, feeling safe that they were venturing on together.

The sky was a solid light-blue highlighting the white clouds huddled throughout the sky, bubbling next to one another so that they were close yet not touching.

*

Kaya spotted a few women with horses outside a circular building structure. Kaya left Orion near the other horses, grabbed her essential saddlebag and walked into what appeared to be a bathhouse. In Syene, she would go to the bathhouse with Arius.

This one was only for women. There was one large circular tub with steaming water from the hot stones within. Three women were lounging around the edge of the tub chatting.

Kaya peeled off her clothes and stepped into the tub with her lotus essential oil in hand. As she made her way down the steps, she felt tingles from the heated water bubbling up her body.

She sat on the ledge and leaned her head back against the edge of the tub. She rubbed some oil between her hands then tapped the area underneath her eyes, lightly, using her fingertips, making her way up and around her eyes, then down along the sides of her face. She sat up straight and massaged the top of her head with her fingers, until she reached the nape of her neck, then circled around her shoulders. She grabbed her thighs, gently yet firmly, and made her way down each of her legs until she reached her feet. She crossed one leg over the other, and rubbed the tips of each toe using her thumbs in a circular motion, then drew lines upwards along the inside of her foot, and did the same to the other side.

Peace is home to a body, mind and soul in harmony

*

The moon was half-lit behind the trees at a secluded area near the river. Kaya decided to stop there. The river of destruction had become her constant sanctuary.

There was a breeze. The weather had been getting cooler as they moved along land with ripened crops.

Chapter 8

Kaya slept under the naked sky – as the river her sanctuary, the ground her place of rest. She had found a home within nature.

Kaya caught a glimpse of the bright orange streaks of sunrise before quickly falling back asleep.

She was in that familiar state. The waking sleep. She focused on her mind's eye, suddenly bringing in quick flashes of geometric figures. The Flower of Life warped into different shapes with different colors pulling her deeper and deeper within. She tried to keep track of all the images she was seeing.

She jerked back into her body, sat up, looked around and saw Orion awake and grazing.

In the near distance, Kaya could see Abydos which housed the Osirion Temple belonging to Osiris. He was beloved for teaching their ancestors how to reconnect to Source. His soul returned to the Orion constellation, after which, Kaya and Arius had named their horse.

*

She walked alongside Orion through the temple. As she wandered through, she dragged her hands across the different red granite blocks.

There was one block that caught her attention. It had a figure engraved on it, the figure from her sleeping flashes, and the symbol she'd seen one too many times on her journey – the Flower of Life.

She ran the fingers of one hand over it, while clasping her necklace with the other.

Life is filled with wonders.
Start inside.

*

Kaya and Orion were heading out to the river when they noticed swarms of people and skiffs, boats that were made of papyrus reeds, further up. They walked towards them.

Kaya saw a fisherman who was desperately begging to trade his skiff for a horse. It had a yellowish-orange carving of the evil eye on it, which also meant protection in their culture.

"Is everything okay?" she asked the fisherman.

"My wife will be going into labor soon, but she has motion sickness and has been sick from the river. We need to make it to Alexandria or they both won't make it," he said worriedly looking over at his pale wife who sat up against a tree.

"All I have is this boat and we are looking for a horse to trade. Please ma'am, I don't know where you're headed, but if you were to be so kind as to lend us your horse, we could trade back once we reach Alexandria."

Alexandria – The City of Scholars, she thought to herself recalling her husband's words. She hadn't considered going there before.

"I have no idea where I'm headed either." She smiled, trying to make light of the situation.

"Just take care of him. How can I find you in Alexandria?" she asked as she patted Orion.

"Thank you so much! I wish I had more words to show my appreciation for your kindness."

Kaya could tell his sincerity from his humble and soft eyes.

"Once you reach the docks where the boats are, ask one of the fishermen for the dark-green door. They'll be able to direct you instantly!"

The fisherman helped Kaya load her saddlebags onto the boat and gave her directions to follow on the downstream river. Kaya kept a few saddlebags filled with food for the man and his wife. The man helped his wife onto Orion. She smiled faintly at Kaya and mouthed a "thank you" as she clasped Kaya's hands together.

As they rode away the man called out from behind him, "We never got your name!"

"Kaya!" She yelled back.

It was too late for her to ask for theirs. They rode off into the distance leaving Kaya more alone, yet more confident, than when she had first started.

Part 4

Chapter 9

Kaya enjoyed rowing the boat and being on the river by herself. She and Arius had a skiff back home. When she would need some alone time, Kaya would take their skiff out onto the river and spend the entire day reconnecting with herself.

They would separately venture out in search of solitude and peace. When they would arrive home, they revealed their whereabouts and shared their realizations, finding comfort and wisdom in their separateness. They respected each other's need for space.

Maybe those were our Reconciliation Journeys.

"Our communion can hold your mystery, my mystery and our mystery," Arius would say.

She parked the boat on land using it as her bed. Kaya looked up at the moon that was more than half lit yawning after the recollection of their memories.

She spotted the constellation that looked like a pot with three stars outlining the handle and another four stars creating the corners of the container.

"The handle to my pot," she heard Arius say to her as she nodded off to sleep.

*

There were scholars sitting in a circle. Books all around a dark lab. Realizing it was her dream, Kaya focused her energy onto the center between her eyes, immediately flashing into a blank screen and seeing symbols of triangles and circles with lines, crosses and curves.

Chapter 10

When Kaya woke, she looked around at the city which she had been unable to see in the darkness the night before. It had white mud brick walls. She had reached Memphis.

A priestess was sitting at the edge of the river in front of Kaya. She had long, black braided hair. At the top of her head was a gold headpiece with delicate gold threads that ran intricately through her braid, securing the bottom of her braid. She was wearing a gold embroidered piece that covered her bosoms and wrapped around her upper arms with a matching skirt slit on the side.

"It's yours," she almost whispered in a soft tone while turning with a goblet in hand.

The priestess who had seemingly black eyes looked deeply into Kaya's.

Kaya walked towards the woman in confusion and took a seat next to her. The sun shone on the priestess revealing her glimmering light-brown eyes.

She continued looking into Kaya's eyes, "You're journeying into your Inner Cosmos."

The priestess pulled out an object from under one of her upper arm cuffs. It was an ankh, a cross-key with a loop at the top and serpent coiled around it.

She reached out for Kaya's hand and looked deep into her eyes again, as if reaching into her soul.

"You will meet the Wise Men," she prophesied while placing the ankh into Kaya's hand and then clasping Kaya's fingers shut around it.

"Who are the Wise Men?" Kaya asked, mesmerized, but the priestess stood up, turned her back and walked away saying over her shoulder, "Some things are only known to yourself. All you need to do is trust, my dear."

Unknown abundance yet somehow directed connection

Kaya added the ankh to the necklace around her neck.

*

On the boat later that day, Kaya thought about the priestess while she stared out at the river.

The sun was setting over The Great Pyramid to her left, giving the solid stone mass an illuminated, white shining presence from the limestone. She decided to stop there, drawn in by its energy.

She tied the boat to a post and walked to The Great Pyramid. When she entered, there were no lanterns, but her inner light seemed to emulate the pyramid's leading her down a narrow hall to the middle of the pyramid.

A cave door opened to a hidden chamber. When she entered, the door shut behind her. She tried to leave but was unable to open the door of the chamber. Frightened, panic began setting in.

She turned around and noticed a small hole in the cave ceiling. It was bringing in light from the outside. The rays created a larger circle of light on the ground beneath the hole. She walked into the sphere of light, closed her eyes and raised her head towards the light coming from above. She focused on the center between her two eyes suddenly basking into her mind's inner darkness.

There were little dots that morphed into a starry night sky. The stars began twirling clockwise into a galactic spiral. Moving through time and space. Quickly. Hastily. At the speed of light. She rocketed through feeling her breath every time she inhaled.

What am I?

The sound of a cave door opening jolted her back from her astral journey. When she opened her eyes, she could no longer see the sphere of light. The opening in the ceiling had closed.

When she made her way out of the pyramid, she looked up at the sky and noticed the three stars of Orion's Belt, part of the Orion constellation, perfectly aligned with the three main pyramids.

The eye within is the portal to the stars

She had experienced how the night unblanketed souls revealing their Inner Cosmos.

Although it was dark, Kaya decided to continue on the boat through the night. She wrapped her communion blanket around her with the oars tucked closely by as the lantern spread its light on the ripples of the water's surface.

Chapter 11

Kaya realized she had approached what the fisherman had called The Mouth of the Delta, where the river spread out and drained into the sea. She recognized the different streams resembling the canopy of a tree.

She peered out into the strip of river that was glowing from the sun's reflection, remembering the fisherman's directions to keep on the far left.

The ocean was beginning to swallow up the narrow river. It was Kaya's first time seeing the ocean. The water turned from a murky green to a clearer turquoise near the coast.

There were people huddled around the harbor. She found a small space between two smaller boats and squeezed between them.

When she tied the boat to a post, she recalled the fisherman telling her to ask about a green door.

She asked a person near her, but he unintentionally ignored her preoccupied with untying his skiff. She asked another person who was seated peacefully on the edge of the dock. He pointed towards a nearby small alley motioning to keep straight.

*

The alley had similar wooden brown doors, but when she reached the very end of the street, she spotted the dark-green door. She wondered whether it was the only street in the area that had such a door since the stranger on the dock was quick to direct her.

She knocked twice and then heard hurried footsteps approaching from the other side.

Once it opened, she saw that it was the fisherman.

"Kaya! You made it!" he exclaimed, welcoming her with gleaming eyes.

"Come meet our daughter," he said eagerly leading her up the stairs to a room where his wife was sitting cradling her newborn.

"She's beautiful," Kaya whispered, taking the child into her arms, rocking her back and forth gently.

"Her name is Kaya," the woman said.

Kaya's eyes smiled behind some tears. She had met this couple only for a split second not realizing the impact she had made in their lives.

"You're blessed with such a wonderful family, Gennadios and Maia," she said smiling at the man and woman.

They looked up at her delighted that she had known their names while also acknowledging their interconnectedness.

Part 5

Chapter 12

Kaya was happy to reunite with Orion. He looked healthy and well-tended, his cream coat shining in the light.

They made their way into the city. The City of Scholars. Arius had told her tales about the alchemists here. He was very fond of their work, transmuting base metal into gold – an inner transformation reflected outward.

She reached a white building with pillars holding a triangular piece at the top. The Great Library of Alexandria.

Behind the building there was a garden. Kaya tied Orion to one of the posts and entered a reddish wooden back door leading to an open courtyard.

She saw six men sitting around a table drinking tea. They were all dressed in white himations almost matching their whitish-grey beards. They looked at Kaya welcomingly surprised.

"Kaya, come sit," she heard a voice saying.

She turned to locate the voice. It was the old man from the cave. She sat on the empty seat around the table facing the old man.

"Kaya has traveled here from Syene," the old man continued.

"Syene?" one of the other men asked, his face expressing the horror of its destruction. "The flood from a few weeks ago wiped out the entire land."

"Yes. I was lucky enough to have fled from there," Kaya replied quietly, looking down at her fingers which were in her lap playing with one another.

"Welcome dear. We're happy that you could make it here."

When she looked up, Kaya saw one of the other men who had a powerful yet graceful presence.

"I want to know the way of transmutation," she said to the old man from the cave.

The men looked around at each other.

The old man asked the other men to leave, all but the man who had a powerful presence.

"My name is Solon," the older man said, finally introducing himself. "And this is Zosimos."

He pointed at the peaceful bald man with a receding hairline across the back of his head. His brown intense eyes seemed to hold the world's wisdom and secrets, the mystical and esoteric, having seen the unseen.

Kaya recollected the names from the mirror. It was her name among the group.

"We have a lodging for you in that corner." Solon pointed to a hallway to the right of a staircase.

"The rooms here are accommodations for the Sages. Up those stairs, you will enter the Great Library. This quarter is off limits to everyone apart from the Sages living here. The food hall is in that room to the left of the staircase. We have breakfast, lunch and dinner there. If you need anything at all, please do let me know. We're your family now."

Solon then stood up and accompanied her to her lodge. They walked past the right of the staircase into a narrow hall. There were seven doors on the right side of the wall. Her lodge was at the very end.

It was a cave-like room equipped with a small wooden bed with folded linen on top and a small round table with a few stools around it. The kitchenette had a tiny storage area with teas, juices, vegetables and fruits.

Kaya's favorite part was the window overlooking a garden and from what she could see, a tree stump.

"I believe Orion is with you? Let me show him to the fields," Solon said kindly.

*

That evening, Kaya had some chamomile tea in her garden. The garden beside hers was lit up leaving her wondering which of the men was staying next to her.

As she peeked through the trees separating them, she saw Zosimos seated on a cushion on the grass.

She had hoped it would be him.

Wanting to make his acquaintance, she grabbed an extra terracotta teacup and placed it on the tray with the still hot teapot hoping he would want some.

"Would you like some tea?" she offered, popping her head through an opening in one of the trees.

He pointed to a bush near her. There was a little black gate.

She made her way through to his garden, sat down on the cushion near him and poured some tea.

"Mmm, I haven't had this tea since Arius," he said sipping the flavorful tea.

She looked down at her fingers as she always did when his name came up feeling insecure about not knowing about his past.

Anger traveled through her and she found herself spewing, "How is it that he had a whole life I didn't know about?"

Zosimos let her anger pass through him, understanding her pain yet aloof in his reply, "What life are you talking about?"

His question confused her.

"What other life is there apart from the one he was living?"

"Most people lead two lives. An outer one and an inner one. Only he who is aligned, has but one."

He took in her silence and continued, "The Inner Journey is a journey one makes alone. To the unseen or to that which we're afraid to see."

He paused, looking at her inquisitively.

"So the real question is, by blaming Arius for your pain, what are you resisting?"

She stared blankly at him trying to digest his question. Zosimos looked up at the sky as if the answers had been written there. Kaya followed his gaze in search for the answer.

His question echoed in the background as she lost herself in Sirius' burning light.

Chapter 13

Kaya walked by the sea alongside Solon who had been kind enough to accompany her to the port. The mountains barricaded the city on one side, while the ocean hugged the coast on the other.

They walked in silence, listening to the waves rolling into each other. The breeze was refreshing.

Kaya stopped at a staircase feeling drawn to the waters.

"I'm going for a walk on the beach. I'll meet you back at the lodge."

Solon had noticed her fixation as if he had been waiting for her to say those words.

She glided down the white stairs that led to the sandy beach and allowed her feet to sink into the powdery and chalky sand. She sank one foot in front of the other until she reached the water.

The first wave reached the tips of her toes covering her feet. She took off her himation and tossed it on the sand behind her leaving her with her chiton.

She walked deeper in and dived, grateful that Arius had taught her how to swim. Although she had been reluctant at first, he knew how much she loved the water and promised to take her to the ocean if she learned how to swim.

She turned on her back and lay with her arms spread out like a starfish, allowing her hair to flow around her. Her ears were underwater taking in the fullness of the ocean.

The waves passed through her body. Wave by wave, she felt heavy layers being swept away, cleansing her body.

Up above, the clouds moved along. She closed her eyes.

She felt energy build up in her left arm, allowing it to extend outwards. Her hand waded back towards her body, bringing in waves that washed over her heart and womb.

She dipped her head backwards so that she was now entirely underwater before she pulled it back out and stood on her feet.

The horizon between the ocean and sky seemed to collide colorfully mixing together as one.

The heart connects the mind and soul

*

After dinner, Kaya headed to the library in search of a book to read before bed.

There was a whole area assigned to alchemy books. She bent down to look through them and pulled out a scripture by Zosimos of Panopolis called The Book of the Keys of the Work. She flipped through it happy she had come across his work.

Behind the empty space of the book in her hand, she noticed a small hole in the wall with the silhouette of an object.

She placed her hand in the dark hole feeling the hard-dusty object. She pulled it out and wiped the dust off.

It was a green tablet. The Emerald Tablet.

She hid it in her himation and quickly made her way to her lodge. She prepared some tea, lit some candles and sat in her garden trying to decipher the characters on the tablet. There were some symbols she recognized from her dream. The triangles and circles with lines, crosses and curves.

The leaves near the gate rustled, drawing Kaya's attention from the tablet to Zosimos. Surprised by his sudden entry, she had forgotten about the tablet in her hand. As he approached her, Zosimos grinned at what she had found.

Feeling like Zosimos could clear up some of her confusion and accepting that he'd already seen it, she proceeded to ask, "What is this? What do these characters mean?"

"I wouldn't get too caught up with it. The real work is in discovering your demons. We've been taught to be good. The light, the positive, the beautiful, the seen. But what about the bad? The dark, the negative, the ugly, the hidden?"

She looked down at the tablet now recognizing a phrase that she hadn't before.

"As above, so below. As within, so without."

Zosimos was nodding with a gentle smile. Whatever he said always seemed to elicit a deeper knowing response from Kaya although she didn't wholly understand it herself.

"I came to tell you we have a ceremony tomorrow. Be ready by sunrise. Be sure to get some rest."

She wanted to ask where they would be going but decided not to. She looked up at the sky noticing the bright full moon.

Chapter 14

Kaya woke before the break of dawn to return the Emerald Tablet to its little nook then sat in the courtyard with some tea.

The men arrived one by one until all six of them were there. Solon was in the center of the room when he began leading the way to the wall behind the staircase near the hall to Kaya's room.

There was a camouflaged opening in the rocky wall that she hadn't noticed before. The door led to a bricked hallway. At the end was a locked gate.

Solon unlocked the gate and waited behind letting the rest in before him. They entered a chamber with seven multicolored mosaic doors.

Each of the men stepped in front of a door, pulled out his ankh and placed it in a small opening, allowing the door to open.

Kaya placed her hand around her neck, clasping the ankh that the woman on the river had given her.

Solon pointed at the middle door and nodded, signaling her to proceed, while also confirming that it was the key to use.

Kaya took off her necklace and placed the ankh in the keyhole. The door opened. As soon as she stepped through, the door closed behind her.

She walked into a dark lab-like room, lit by rays of candlelight. The men were seated on mats on the floor around the candles aligned in the shape of a pentagram.

Kaya made her way to an opening near Zosimos and sat down.

The men were quiet. They all placed their hands on their heart, closed their eyes and bowed, clasping their two hands together. She closed her eyes and followed the men's hand gestures. Her mind attuned to the collective sound of quietness.

They took deep breaths into their hearts, feeling the air detoxifying their bodies.

Growing lighter with each breath, they transcended into floating entities forming a single greater presence.

We are one
We are whole
Seeing from the inside
Awake within
I see you through me

Suddenly, there was a loud bell. A single chime.

Their souls returned to their bodies bringing back their awareness to this realm separating them from their vastness and returning them to their earthly containers.

Their eyes slowly opened from their awakened slumber, adjusting to their surroundings. Their faces radiated with love, light and peace.

Time and space ceased to exist during their meditation.

The men got up and Kaya followed them towards a wooden door at the back.

The door opened out into a forest that had seven tiny cabins surrounding a metal cauldron fire pit. There was the smell of burning sage. On a wooden table, there was mountain tea, a healing herb, as well as water, juices, figs, grapes and dates.

Kaya ate some dates and then sat on one of the mats near Solon. "How often do these ceremonies take place?"

"On the full moon. Welcome to your Integration Ceremony my dear."

*

Each cabin had a single bed with a bathroom. There was a set of white linen pants with a matching shirt placed on each of the beds.

Kaya had put on her pair and was ready to go to bed when she heard a knock on her door.

Zosimos popped his head into her cabin and said, "Come outside."

The ceremony would go on.

Barefoot, Kaya walked out onto the soil and, again, joined the men standing in a circle around the unlit fire pit.

When Zosimos stood in front of the pit, its flames seemed to suddenly flare, dancing to the sounds of the nay flute and harp.

They closed their eyes and went in.

In.

In.

In.

Deeper and deeper.

She felt an intensity of energy flaring throughout her body with the appearance of the rattling sistrum. Her hips moved bewitchingly to the sound of the melodic instruments and the flicker of the fire pit. She slowly outlined the air with her swaying body, twirling and raising her arms up and over her head, crossing them over one another, the energy dictating her body, allowing it to take control.

Their eyes were still closed as they continued to sway. To let go. To release. Inhaling the melody and exhaling the dance. They were dancing souls, listeners and receivers, with syncing bodies, climactic melodies and flaming fires. Eyes shut, while their bodies surrendered, minds listened, and hearts smiled.

It started to rain.

Kaya collapsed on the floor. The water dripped all over her hair, face and body. With each splash, she released her own tears.

She sat up cross-legged, ran both her hands through her hair and looked up at the sky, feeling embedded with the dark and light.

The flicker of light from the firepit caught her attention and brought her back to the cauldron which was now burning out.

Someone grazed her shoulder and placed their hand gently there.

It was Solon.

She forgot about the other Sages, yet, she was able to sense their togetherness throughout the ceremony.

Solon took her hand and walked her to her cabin. Exhausted after having been up since the last sunrise, she fell onto her bed with her arms spread out and drifted off to sleep.

Part 6

Chapter 15

Kaya woke up by midafternoon feeling like she could sleep more but instead planted her feet on the ground and got herself onto the porch for some tea, wanting to process the Integration Ceremony.

Zosimos walked up the porch steps and sat on the chair next to her bearing a tray of mountain tea.

"It feels like ever since I've set out on this journey, things within me have awakened, like I've aligned," Kaya started immediately while reaching for a cup of tea.

"You have aligned. You've awakened the Creator within you."

"Why me?"

"Because you chose it. It's as simple as that. A person can choose whether they want to return to Source. We all have a guide within us. All we need to do is listen."

"Wouldn't everyone choose that?"

"The Inner Journey is tumultuous and painful, as you may have experienced. It starts with The Dark Night of the Soul, a deconstruction of everything you once knew, in order to shine a mirror on your inner darkness. But each pain comes with its own remedy, so only through that darkness, will you find light. Solve et Coagula. The Emerald Tablet you found simply outlines the steps of this process which is already known within us."

He paused, taking a sip of his tea.

"And the result is the Philosopher's Stone, an inner integration to a state of wholeness." He smiled, looking at her necklace.

She clasped her necklace and looked down at it. The Flower of Life symbol, once copper, was now gold.

"And the symbols?"

"They're sacred imprints. Think of them as universal truths, codes, manifesting into creation."

Kaya took a deep breath trying to digest all the information.

"I want to stay here in the woods for a while." She sighed, looking around. "Would I be able to stay in this cabin?"

Zosimos looked at Kaya, smiling as he did when he aligned with her ideas. "There's another one that will be more fitting for you. Come, let's grab your belongings from the lodge first."

*

After collecting her belongings, they rode Orion deeper into the woods until they reached two trees that had connecting branches and leaves, intertwined in a circle. Cradled between the two trees, there was a pond, with lily pads and loti scattered around. A cute, cozy cabin nestled just behind.

"Who does this belong to?" Kaya asked, mesmerized.

"Well, this whole plot of land belongs to the library, so Solon. But this patch of land and this cabin are yours."

Kaya looked at Zosimos perplexingly.

"Your late husband bought this for you."

She felt a warm rush of energy permeating her body.

Did Arius experience similar rituals? Did he experience his own awakening?

Before she let the flood of questions overtake her mind, she made her way to the cabin door.

*

That night, Kaya sat on a swing that was hung on the tangled tree and looked up at the less than full moon. Orion lay on the grass with his head stretched out over her lap.

She had found her home and realized that her husband was right. She was guided.

Part 7

Chapter 16

The familiar high-pitched whistling sound woke her up as a ray of light hit her face, spreading its warmth through her. Opening her eyes, she smiled at the sight of the eagle who was perched on the branch near her window.

She walked outside of her cabin to one of the intertwined trees, excited to start her day meditating. She sat down, leaned on the trunk and dug her feet into the ground, rooting herself.

Like the tree, her trunk frolicked, pulsating with energy, drawing in magnitudes of electrical currents from her roots, branching out and spreading the waves through her to the world, while her green leaves bloomed with creation. But sometimes, her trunk slowed down as her orange and red leaves withered, her roots preserved what was left of her energy, while her naked branches protected her exposed skin.

She crossed her legs, one over the other, closed her eyes, clasped her hands together and bowed. She had learned the gesture signified the union of body, mind and soul.

She focused on the center between her eyes as she did in her sleep journeys. When she fixated on the black screen, she saw a big bursting ball of light in a dark space. She was dipped in dark navy water, drawing in light from Source.

Her heart began racing as she noticed a presence near her.

Arius was also dipped in water.

She was unsure whether she was dreaming, imagining or whether she was experiencing this in some other realm.

She began to cry but noticed that the more emotional she became, the more the emotion returned her back to the physical realm.

She took deep breaths to center herself.

Her husband came closer to her, cupping her cheek the way he always did. His touch helped her relax into the palm of his hand. He caressed her face as they looked deeply into each other's eyes. He planted a kiss on her forehead jolting her back to the bark of the tree.

She cried and cried and cried. The floodgates opened.

She felt plucked away from one home, yet whole in another. She realized that faraway place was within her.

She wiped her face and then hugged herself while her hands caressed her arms.

She flashbacked to the beginning of her journey, remembering how she was curled up on the sand dune, homeless, and feeling a defeated surrender. Now, she had found a home, feeling light and whole, a trusting surrender.

She walked towards the cliff, peering out over the lighthouse that Zosimos had pointed out to her the night before. He had told her that, "It shines its light on the shadows of the mind."

Part 8

Chapter 17

Kaya climbed over the roots of the hugging trees, stripping off her white nightgown so that she was naked and slipped into the pond making her way through the loti.

Like the lotus, she grew in adversity, darkness and hardship. And like the lotus, her petals outshone the murky water.

The water covered her entire body, bit by bit, until she was completely submerged. The water was deeper than she had thought.

She stayed underneath, listening to the bubbling echoes. Zosimos' question from her first night at the lodging came back to her.

By blaming Arius for your pain, what are you resisting?

She stuck her head out of the water, her hair falling gracefully behind her.

She lay on her back with her hands spread out freely and her legs close together. She marveled at the sky above. The brightest star cradled into the crescent moon.

The waves passed through her effortlessly as she remembered her encounter with Arius, realizing that, up until that moment, she hadn't paid much attention to the form they had both taken.

Her body felt light, weightless. She was unable to feel either of her legs, or perhaps, felt like they had come together as one.

Myself – I was resisting myself.

About the Author

Sahar Hadid is a Jordanian and Lebanese writer. She was born in Beirut where she spent most of her youth. Her own life mirrors that of her character Kaya, as she had started on her inner journey when she went to university in Madrid, Spain. She began journaling about her self-discoveries as well as writing poetry. Currently Sahar continues to write and teach, as she values knowledge using it to contribute to the world around her.

CPSIA information can be obtained
at www.ICGtesting.com
Printed in the USA
BVHW040942060423
661869BV00016B/1099

9 789948 802273